THE SWORDSMAN'S TALE

The Early Years

ZENODAMUS

Synopsis

In late nineteenth-century British India, the Swordsman is recruited and groomed by the Order of the Wolves to battle a cunning and deadly enemy. At stake are India's cultural heritage and the fight for its independence.

Against the backdrop of the third-highest mountain in the world, Kanchenjunga, *The Early Years* chronicles the transformative journey of a sheltered boy of unknown origin becoming the formidable Swordsman who wields his sword against General Dier, a mass murderer, and Louis Short, a cannibal with metal teeth.

The Swordsman's Tale, a novella by Zenodamus, is the window to a universe where spirituality combines with martial arts, pristine forests hold centuries-old secrets, anecdotes carry a dose of magical realism, and ancient philosophies guide the moral compass.

ACKNOWLEDGEMENT

A big thank-you to all those who made this book
possible!

x

Disclaimer

All the characters in this book are fictional. Any resemblance to a person living or dead is coincidental.

Intellectual Property

PROLOGUE

I, Zenodamus, have traveled to various parts of the world to seek the meaning of life. During my journey through the mountains of the subcontinent, I encountered a storm that cut all types of transportation and forms of communication. I took refuge at an ancient monastery, devoting my time at its library. In the archives, I discovered old documents, among which were the memoirs of the Swordsman.

Because of the nature of his activities and spiritual inclination, the Swordsman decided to remain anonymous. Much like true heroes, he preferred to avoid glory and remain in oblivion. After reading his memoirs, I decided to bring his astonishing stories to life. This book attempts to chronicle his early years.

Zenodamus

NORTHEAST INDIA

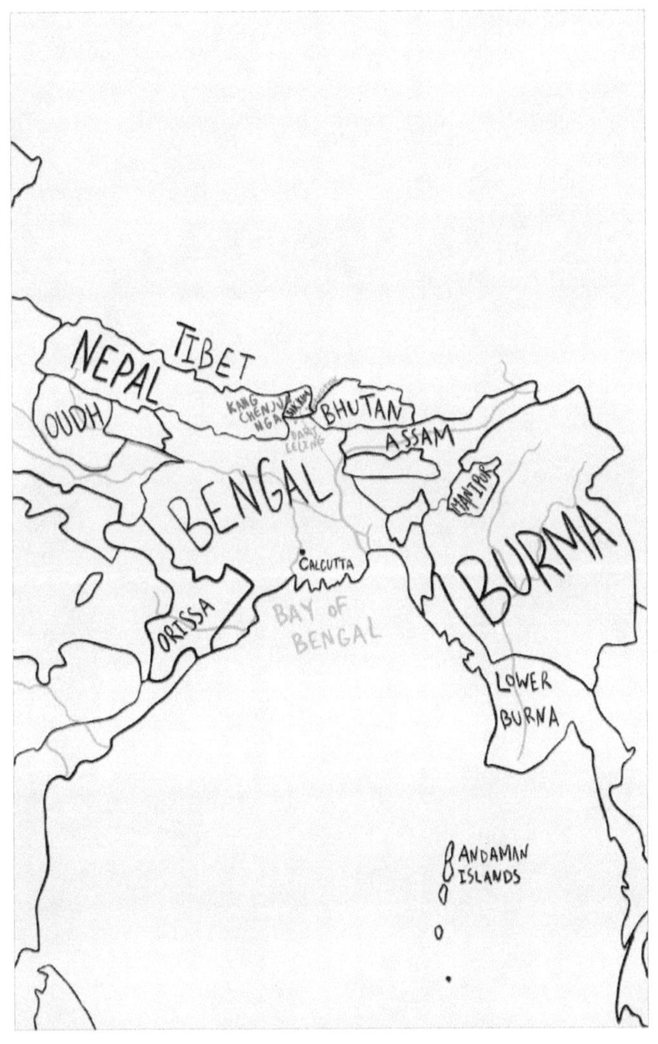

PRINCIPIUM

1

I do not know my origin. I was only a few months old when a kind-hearted couple discovered me nestled at the base of a tree in the forest. On that fateful day, as twilight settled in, the wolves transmitted a cryptic message from deep inside the forest, hypnotizing the atmosphere with their howls. The couple approached the bend on the road where the tree was. Once they heard my infantile wailing, the horse cart was stopped.

"Someone appears to be at peril," the wife exclaimed.

"We must investigate," replied the husband.

Holding a lantern that made a feeble attempt to light the path, the couple tracked my cries to the tree where I lay, clutching a twig like a sword in my hand.

"The child is hungry," the wife spoke, after coming to terms with the horror of witnessing a baby left alone to fight his fate in a howling forest. She rushed to the cart to fetch nourishment. A sip of water brought a smile to my face.

"Whoever left him there must have been in a terrible situation," the husband said.

"We can't leave the child. The wolves may devour him."

"Let's wait here for a while. Someone might come back for him."

"There are no clues to identify the origin of the child."

Time continued to tick by, but there was no sign of anyone showing up. During this tense period, the couple worked to make me laugh. Subconsciously, a bond was forged between us. Much like the twilight on that evening, imperialism was on its last legs in the late nineteenth century. Before it got darker, we rushed back to our village.

2

The village is located in one of the most beautiful parts of the world. It is nestled in a verdant forest that is arranged meticulously on the hilly terrain of Northeast India. To its north are the snowcapped Himalayas, the immovable giants whose mood swings can turn a smile in a far-off village into a frown. On a clear day, we could view the famous Kangchenjunga mountain. Towering over 8,500 meters, it is the third-highest mountain in the world. The hilly terrain and the resulting cool atmosphere serve the region to cultivate the fragrant tea that is highly cherished by tea connoisseurs.

My fascination with swordsmanship continued to flourish. Other kids in the neighborhood played with swords too, therefore, the natural next step for me was to engage in friendly matches with them.

However, the matches did not turn out well for the kids, as they struggled to beat me. The more they lost, the more aggressive they became in trying to win the next contest. The more aggressive they became, the more they suffered at my hands. As days passed, my reputation developed to the point where I was simply referred to as "the Swordsman," the name that I would carry for the rest of my life.

In the evenings, we meandered the cobbled streets to the village square where "the huge, old tree" stood. The circumference of the tree was wrapped with a bench constructed of stones. The grand "huge, old tree" had an equal in Hariram, the village intellectual, who sat on the bench as if it were his throne and imparted wisdom to us through well-crafted stories. The village square was our wonderland.

The village often speculated on Hariram's age. He appeared to have been present in the village ab aeterno. With a forehead that was busy with wrinkles, eyebrows that had been allowed to grow wild, and a snow-white beard that stretched to his waist, he appeared to be over a hundred years old. He usually wore an orange robe that covered him from neck to toes. The robe, along with his tall and slim demeanor, gave him the appearance of a saint. If he had had a halo around his head, he would have been an angel.

On an eventful evening, Hariram proclaimed, "We are under the British Raj (Rule)." Enchanted by the world of swords and sheltered by my parents, I had not delved into matters such as who ruled who, and why it should matter, when people are usually ruled by someone anyway.

Hariram explained, "The British came from an island in the west called Britain, traveling across the long and deep seas to trade with Hindustan (India). Later, the natives gave the East India Company permission to set up trading posts. To protect the trading posts, the company raised an army. With time, the army grew powerful enough to topple local rulers. Eventually, the company became the ruler of most of Bharat (India)."

On that evening, we learned that in 1857, the native Hindustani soldiers of the British Army revolted against the British company. The bullets used in the Enfield rifles were wrapped up in a material that was rumored to have been spawned from cows and pigs. Before firing the bullet, a soldier had to unwrap the cartridge with his mouth, creating conditions that sparked religious insensitivity. The situation ultimately led to the revolt, which is commonly referred to as the Sepoy Mutiny.

To crush the mutiny, the company resorted to brutal tactics. Some punishments involved tying up a soldier in front of a cannon to blow him up. The more unfortunate ones were hanged from a tree until they took their last breath. Because of this revolt, Queen Victoria officially transferred the business in India to the hands of the crown. In 1877, the Queen proclaimed herself the Empress of India. The subcontinent became the shiniest jewel in her crown.

After Hariram finished the story, he opened the floor for questions.

"How did our village fall to the British?"

"The British introduced 'Doctrine of Lapse,' where if the ruler died without an heir, the British could take control of the state."

"What happened to the heir?"

Hariram scratched his head. "When the baby prince was traveling with his mother through the forest, their caravan was slain by bandits, who spoke in a foreign dialect. The remains of the prince were not discovered among the carnage. It is believed that the wolves in the forest might have taken him away. A month later, our king passed away in a horse-riding accident. Therefore, we migrated to the British flag."

The evening scurried to night. As we headed back to our homes, the cold breeze from the mountains percolated our bodies. Over the next few years, we continued to be enlightened on such news and stories from Hariram. These stories were one of the ways through which we discovered the world.

3

Wolves are magical and mysterious. They are revered by the villagers for their bravery and teamwork. For reasons unknown to me, wolves appear in my dreams. One day, I had a dream, or what some may refer to as a vision: In a dark forest, I was running away from someone. Blood was dripping from my body. Unable to run farther, I rested at a tree. As I began to lose consciousness, I heard a wolf howl. It was not threatening but protecting me. When I opened my eyes, I discovered a large wolf towering over me. It smiled and beckoned me to follow it, a command that I obeyed without hesitation.

Startled by the dream, I sprang up from the bed to discover Hariram engaged in a conversation with my parents. "What would have caused Hariram to visit us in the morning?" I thought out loud. The three of them arrived at an agreement after a prolonged discussion. Hariram entered my room and asked me to pack my bags. He said firmly, "It is time for you to get further education and training. Everything has been arranged, so there is no point in arguing." When Hariram ordered firmly, no one in the village argued with him anyway.

In the evening, my parents took me to a fortune-teller. She was an old gypsy. There were stories of her flying in from the high mountains that went farther from Nepal and into Tibet. It was also believed that she was older than Hariram. That anyone could be older than the old Hariram was difficult to fathom. The late king and queen used to visit her for advice too.

The fortune-teller lived in a hut at the outskirts of the village. A narrow stream ran next to her hut, ensuring that a wide assortment of flora thrived to make the area fragrant. We rode in a horse cart on the sinuous road, passing a variety of houses. Huts, large mountain homes with long, slanting roofs, and houses with Tibetan-style resting hill roofs dotted the landscape.

Upon entering the hut, the gypsy gave me a welcoming nod. She smiled at me warmly and asked me to sit in front of her. I had expected to see a crystal ball but was disappointed to not find one. She remarked, "Ah, you are about to go on a long journey."

After we settled in her hut, she explained that we are all influenced by our destiny and karma, telling the famous story of the woodcutter and the hunter. The woodcutter slayed a tree to sell the wood to a hunter, who crafted it into a potent arrow. On a hunting mission, the hunter mistook the woodcutter for prey, fired that arrow at him, and then hurried to fetch his prize. However, fate dictated the tree, which the woodcutter had been cutting, to dislodge and crush the hunter. The incidence left no survivors. Our karma guides our destiny too.

She asked me to reveal my palms. As she studied them in detail, her smile vanished. She took some oil from a container next to her and rubbed it on my palms, while also pinching specific areas on them. Once she was satisfied that every line on the palms had been unearthed and deciphered, she signaled me to withdraw. She contemplated for a few moments and gathered the courage to remark gravely in a poetic style. We found the poem difficult to understand.

She said:

"A time will come when you will be at sea. Your sword will be under the sting of the bee. After dusk, comes dawn. You will sing like a swan."

Mesmerized by this hypnotic session, we headed back to our home. Since I was departing on the journey, my parents had prepared my favorite dishes for dinner. I feasted on a bowl of sweet and sour tomato soup. Roti (Bharati bread) and deliciously cooked spicy potatoes were served to be enjoyed with a large glass of buttermilk. For dessert, there was rice pudding decorated with royal raisins and almonds. That night, I went to bed elated.

4

At dawn, we were interrupted by army bugles. The village was raided by British troops commanded by one General Raymond Dier, who was an archetypical villain displaying racial prejudice and imperial stubbornness. He wore a bushy moustache, which juxtaposed with his small, cold, blue eyes. A mere glance at him could convince anyone that General Dier meant business.

General Dier summoned the villagers to gather at the square. A Hindustani drafted as a British soldier announced that a railway line was to pass through the village. The Raj would require land for it. The villagers were to provide the land, for which they would receive nominal compensation. The railway line was to serve a greater good, as it would bring prosperity to the village. And prosperity brings happiness for all.

On one hand, General Dier believed that the natives abhorred the British because they promoted progress and discipline to these lands. He was bitter at the ingratitude shown by the natives and would not hesitate to use a firm hand to achieve his goals. On the other hand, the villagers knew of the story of a devil who enchanted its potential victims with promises of prosperity and a better future to own their souls. In the future, politicians too would use this particular trick to gain votes. The modus operandi is to promise prosperity to the voters, but in reality, only keep it for themselves. The voters would remain dilapidated but continue to dream of a better future.

The villagers respected their land, which had passed hands from one generation to the next. They were emotionally tethered to it. Moreover, prosperity is subjective. What was prosperous for the Raj might not have been prosperous for the natives. The villagers believed that material wealth is not the sole path to happiness. The ability to respect what one has and search for joy in that was priceless to them. In the future, in pursuit of material happiness, human beings would not only hijack the planet, forgetting that it was designed for all types of flora and fauna, but also put it in a precarious state.[i] Would transforming the moon into junk be our next mission? These villagers had the clairvoyance to not be led into a vicious cycle. They protested.

To counter the protest, the British made another announcement. General Dier claimed that a deadly plague had hit the region. As a precautionary measure, the villagers were to be examined. Infected individuals would be quarantined and immediately shifted to a camp for treatment.

Villagers whose lands were required for the railway line were quarantined. Among the doomed ones, heading to the camp, were my parents. General Dier announced that food and other basic items would be provided. Post lunch, the healthy villagers felt sick. They were marched to tents where they tumbled into a deep sleep, never to wake up again.

A fire engulfed the camp, reducing the dormant villagers to dust and ashes. The village suspected this to be an act of arson, but General Dier termed it as an unfortunate accident. Since the obstacles to the railway line had magically vanished, the work on it was to commence soon. Undoubtedly, General Dier was a man who hid three aces up his sleeves.

After the tragedy, Hariram took me under his wing. He understood my despair and comforted me. At some point, I realized that the tears in my eyes had vanished. I was not sure if I had exhausted them or if the fire that General Dier had ignited deep inside me made the tears evaporate. And then came the time to embark on the journey.

5

We saddled the horses and crisscrossed the hilly terrain to head to a plateau located at the north of the village. As for my luggage, its most substantial part was my sword. Hariram had asked me to pack light. He had advised, "You will be provided with the things you need." At a distance, I heard the wolves howl, as if to wish bon voyage.

Hariram was a master of navigating terrains using clues provided by nature. He looked for signs on land, in the position of the sun and direction of the wind, and by examining the flora for clues. As we rode, the breeze carried the fragrance from nearby tea gardens to us. We stopped at an ancient temple to pray and seek blessings.

The old temple was a sight to behold. The frame was made of white marble and had a gold border. The elevated floor was stacked on a foundation of heavy stones textured with shapes of weapons such as bows, arrows, swords, and spears. The roof was a tall, brick-red pediment. On top of the roof, an orange triangular swallowtail pennon fluttered with pride. Round columns with musical instruments decoratively crafted into them occupied the space between the floor and the roof. A short flight of wide and tall steps transported visitors to the floor.

To the right of the steps was the idol of Lord Ganesha, whose blessings are auspicious for new ventures. Opposite of Lord Ganesha, to the left of the steps, stood Lord Hanuman, whose blessings protect from harm. We climbed the steps to find priests tied up in lotus position, murmuring the holy syllable, "Om." The priests were oblivious to their surroundings. Their chants created an environment of peace and tranquility in the temple. The main chamber displayed the idol of Lord Ramdevpir, who saddled his favorite green horse whilst holding a spear in his left hand and showering blessings with the raised right hand. Following Lord Ramdevpir on foot was the idol of Harji Bhatti.

This particular idol depicted Lord Ramdevpir with large, bulging eyes. The angry eyes juxtaposed with the smiling lips, creating the effect of both disapproval and approval of our bad and good actions respectively. The hinged door, which led to the main chamber, was made up of iron bars. I opened the door to touch the feet of the Lord to seek his blessing. As I entered the chamber, I discovered a cat trapped inside it. Waiting for the door to open, the cat rushed out. The event served as a signal to break away from my sorrows and enjoy the moment. The visit to the temple not only brought back an element of peace inside me but also brimmed me with confidence to take on the challenge that awaited me.

As we marched on, Hariram said, "The plateau is not far." On the way, Hariram told stories about our region. "In 1855, Nepal and Tibet were at war, which lasted for about a year. Since the two countries could not carry out a sustained campaign, they settled for peace. Post-war, the twelfth Dalai Lama came to power. However, he died under mysterious circumstances while still in his youth. Now, Tibet is guided by the thirteenth Dalai Lama."

As twilight approached, the remaining sun rays bounced off the snowy peak of Kangchenjunga, making it dazzle like a jewel. After arriving at the plateau, Hariram said, "We will rest here for the night. At dawn, the next leg of the journey will commence." We exchanged Shubh Ratri, or Bonne Nuit.

That night, the wolves visited me in my dream. This time, we were running together in the forest. Suddenly, the pack stopped. But, for some reason, I kept on running.

As dawn chased the darkness away and the cool breeze froze time, I sipped a cup of the fragrant tea, observing Hariram search the sky. Maybe he was seeking a specific bird. Suddenly, against the run of play, Hariram's eyes lit up with excitement as he located the bird. As I looked up in the sky, my jaw dropped. A big, orange ball was descending toward us.

"Is that the sun flying toward us?"

"It is a hot air balloon," replied Hariram.

The odd structure glided through the air to position itself above us. I was too shocked to think about what it would do next. Slowly, it started to descend vertically. Attached to the big, orange ball was a basket, from which a figure was waving at us. Hariram responded in kind.

As soon as the orange balloon landed on the plateau, the figure jumped out of the cage. He appeared to be as tall as Hariram but with a beard that extended to his knees. When he bent, the beard swept the ground. Earlier, I met a fortune-teller who was older than Hariram, and now, a man who carried a longer beard. The man wore a turban, and his eyes were wrapped around by a pair of bug-eyed, round glasses. Because of their long beards, the gentlemen appeared identical, creating an illusion of being twins. Both continued to greet each other with enthusiasm, engaging in a bear hug, as if they were long-lost friends. Hariram pointed in my direction. "That's the boy!"

The man's warm smile immediately put me at ease. Hariram said, "This is Jairam, my cousin."

Jairam waved. "Hello Swordsman." To my surprise, Jairam's voice sounded similar to Hariram's too.

Hariram looked at me with sad eyes. Struggling to find the right words, he simply said, "It is time to say bye. You shall continue the journey with Jairam."

The news shocked me. "Why are you leaving us?"

"I have to continue the work in the village. As they say, everyone has his destiny." He winked and rode away.

6

Once Hariram disappeared into the horizon, Jairam attempted to cheer me up. He patted my back and inquired, "Have you traveled in a hot air balloon?"

"I haven't seen one before."

"Let me tell you more about it." With that, Jairam enthusiastically began to enlighten me on the subject.

"That big, orange ball is called the envelope. It is attached to the basket, where the pilot is placed. Between the envelope and the basket are the burners, which are used to heat the air inside the envelope. The warmer air rises in cooler air, forcing the balloon to climb up."

"How does the balloon get down?"

"At the top of the envelope are valves, which when opened drive the hot air out of the envelope. This allows the balloon to descend, or slow down its ascent."

"How do we move horizontally?"

"As the wind blows in different directions at different altitudes, we use the burner and the valve to control the ascent and descent to ride the wind in the direction we want to head to."

"Is the use of hot air balloons widespread?"

"Not as widespread as I would have hoped. It has been over a hundred years since the first one crossed the English Channel."

We hopped into the basket. Jairam performed a final inspection of the equipment, passed a pair of the big, round glasses to me, and turned the burners on. As we began to glide up, my excitement increased. "Which direction are we headed?"

"You can tell me that," Jairam teased me.

"How?"

"Which direction is Kangchenjunga from your village?"

"It is at its north?"

"Now point your right hand to the direction we are headed and point your left hand toward Kanchenjunga. Where is it now?"

"If we assume the direction that we are headed to be north, Kanchenjunga would be at its west. Which means that the direction we assumed to be north is east of our village. We are heading east."

"Sabash!"

We climbed higher. Below, the forest and hills created a mesmerizing visual impact. The region was more beautiful than I had imagined. It felt as if the wind was pulling the balloon with an invisible string, inching it closer to God.

As the clouds began to disperse, I saw an astonishing structure reveal itself magically. From the distance, it created an illusion of hanging in the sky. The structure was built on the crest of a twin-peaked mountain, in a fashion that its roof aligned with the summit. Since the contour of the building blended with its surroundings, it gave the appearance of being a part of the mountain. The path leading toward the structure snaked through the cliff. Certain sections of the path disappeared into caves, re-emerging to continue toward the structure. A slope, below the structure, led to a tiny plateau.

Jairam pointed toward the monastery and remarked, "That is our destination, the Wolf's Den." The closer we got to it, the more humungous it became. The wickedly scenic path on the cliff led to the monastery's main gate, a cave with a mouth shaped like the open jaws of a wolf.

Jairam positioned the hot air balloon above the tiny plateau and descended. Once the balloon was secured, we began to climb the path that snaked through the cliff to the monastery. Jairam cautioned, "Be careful. A misstep could throw you over the cliff. While it is beautiful, it is dangerous." To verify the gravity of the situation, I glanced down into the valley to notice the trees at the bottom to be a long distance away.

We navigated the narrow path carefully. Jairam reminded me, "Haste is waste." The trees in the valley had turned into miniature toys, whispering to be played with. At a short distance was the hanging bridge. As we approached it, the breeze gained in intensity. Jairam gave sharp instructions: "Watch closely on how I cross the bridge. Follow me once I am on the other side."

Jairam grabbed the main ropes at the opposite edges of the bridge. The intense breeze not only made the bridge oscillate like a pendulum, but also Jairam's long beard flutter like a flag. Despite the challenging conditions, Jairam floated across the bridge. Once he reached the other side, he waved at me to follow his footsteps. As I put my foot on the bridge, a sense of excitement burst through my veins. Jairam was amused to see me enjoying the adventure.

We continued to navigate through the tricky cliff, passing through narrow caves, to arrive at the jaws of the wolf, which served as a vestibule. The sharp rocks spread around the mouth gave the cave its teeth. Torches lined on its walls provided illumination. At the far end of the cave, a flight of steps led to a huge door with a round arch at its top.

Inside the monastery, a different world awaited us. It was warm and cozy. The door launched us to a courtyard that was open from above. Multi-level buildings formed its perimeter. The courtyard was buzzing with activity as monks performed their chores. As we stepped inside the monastery, we were greeted with smiles and waves. Jairam said, "Today, you will rest. I will show you to your room." He pointed to a hall straight ahead and continued, "Dinner will be served there. When you hear the bell ring thrice, wait at the dining hall's door. I will come and fetch you."

The ground level housed a temple, a large meeting room, kitchen and dining hall, and quarters that served as offices. The courtyard was a huge garden, housing a variety of trees and plants. The main stairs were located next to the dining hall. On the middle level were a library, meditation halls, meeting rooms, martial arts practice rooms, and classrooms. The upper level was the sleeping quarter. My room had a bed with blankets and a pillow, a writing table, and a chair. Next to the bed was a small table which was big enough to accommodate a water jug and a mug. At the far end of the room was a small window covered with iron bars. The window peeked into the backyard, where a huge bell was mounted at the edge of a precipice. The bell had the ability to not only wake us but also a village. A distant corner in the backyard accommodated a storage building. After looking over my accommodations, I decided to rest. As soon as I lay on the bed, my eyes closed.

The bell announced the dinner time, as promised. I rushed downstairs to meet Jairam. After guiding me into the dining hall, he introduced me to the monks. We took our seats at a long table. Monks in charge of the kitchen served a dinner that consisted of vegetable hotchpotch, baked parsley potatoes, spring onion soup, and buttermilk. Everyone treated me with enthusiasm. Since this was a monastery, many preferred a warm silence. I enjoyed the company.

Post dinner, Jairam took me to the meeting room to meet the Great One, the head monk. The meeting chamber was at the opposite end of the dining hall, across the courtyard and next to the main entrance. A broad double door decorated with a wolf motif welcomed us into the room. An enormous, round table at the center of the room served as its main attraction. On a distinguished chair with the tallest back was seated the Great One, who was the oldest living being that I had ever laid my eyes on. Much like Hariram and Jairam, he had a long, white beard; however, he was taller than those two. He delivered a slow, welcoming nod and beckoned us to take our seats. Jairam sat next to the Great One, while I took the chair next to Jairam.

The Great One opened the meeting by asking me, "How was your journey?"

"It was great. Thank you."

"Have you settled down in your room?"

"Yes, sir."

"I am referred to as the Great One. I lead the Order of the Wolves. Our mission is to improve and safeguard the planet for future generations. We believe in equal rights for all, including flora and fauna, as God has created this planet for everyone and not just for humans. We look to fight injustice as much as we can, within the limitations of our karma and destiny. Currently, we are opposed to the British Raj, which is carrying out atrocities on the natives, and the Hindustanis who help the British to subjugate other Hindustanis. Our goal is to ignite the movement to free Bharat of these oppressors."

The Great One paused to see if I had questions. When I didn't, he continued, "Once the British depart, we want to create a state that respects everything that our planet has. Everything has its purpose. We want a system where fifty percent of the land is reserved for wildlife and forests. This helps to maintain the ecosystem. We also want to develop a population that is responsible and respects both nature and all living beings. If we do not shape the region correctly, it will eventually become overpopulated and polluted. We do not want to create a misguided population that neither cares for a higher purpose nor achieves anything except short term self-interest."

Jairam added, "We seek individuals who can carry the movement forward. You were identified as one who can bring value to the Order of the Wolves. We will keep you at the monastery for the next few years to master disciplines such as philosophy, languages, basic science and math, and martial arts. After your training, we will give you missions that can drive positive changes."

The Great One remarked, "But first, we have to know your wish. Would this interest you?"

Ever since I stepped on the hot air balloon, I had sensed that I was being guided by my destiny. I replied, "Yes, sir."

"Please be advised that this is not an easy path to embark upon. You will need a strong will, discipline, and focus to complete this journey."

"I am committed, sir."

"Jairam is the head of our teachers. He has created a schedule for you. Welcome aboard and good luck."

"Thank you, sir."

The Great One left the chamber. Jairam continued to explain the program and the schedule to me. Over the next few years, I engrossed myself in various subjects to be reborn as a new person.

ILLUSTRATIO

7

Japan remained under military rule for almost 700 years, first transitioning to it in 1192, when Minamoto Yoritomo crushed his enemies to be appointed as the shogun. Fifteenth- to sixteenth-century Japan hovered in relative chaos and fractured into independent states. The constant wars among these states helped the samurai class to gain prominence. The year 1603 marked the beginning of the Edo period, where Japan united again under the shogun. This led to a period of relative peace, where the samurai class began to lose its luster. In 1868, Japan decided to topple the Togiwaka government and restored power to Emperor Meiji, marking the end of the Edo period and the beginning of the end of the samurai era.

Toshiro Wakayama was a samurai. Later, he turned into a ronin, and then developed a desire to delve into Buddhist and Hindu philosophies. Around the mid-nineteenth century, he left Japan, tracked through China, and rested at Tibet, where he encountered Jairam. Their interaction revealed a common interest in spirituality and martial arts. At Jairam's insistence, the Great One allowed him to recruit Toshiro to the Order of the Wolves.

Toshiro, a short man with a ponytail, was often found wearing dark blue kimonos, creating a contrast with the orange robes of other monks. When not wielding his swords, he devoted his time to the library, where he meticulously studied ancient books. He had also become fluent in Hindustani. I honed the art and science of swordsmanship under the masterful direction of Toshiro Wakayama.

Toshiro evaluated me to make me aware of the "unknown unknowns" in my swordsmanship. From someone who wielded one sword, he turned me into one who wielded two—long (core) and short (companion) swords, to both attack and defend.

Fighting with two swords, one in each hand, allows the arms and body to maneuver more freely, creating the difference between delivering a fatal blow and a scratch. The long sword provides reach, while the short one utilizes narrow spaces and turns into the striking force in close combat. Other benefits include the ability to distract the opponent with one sword while striking with the other. When held in the cross position, the swords turn into a shield.

Besides the ability to fight other swordsmen, I acquired the skill to fight opponents who used other weapons. Toshiro often remarked to me, "If you mastered the art of fighting with two swords, you could become unstoppable."

Much like Hariram, Jairam taught intellectual subjects. Under his direction, I learned how to navigate by using nature. Jairam also taught philosophy, literature, and history. In one of the classes, we discussed magic and science. The discussion stemmed from an event referenced in Ramayana, where a bridge is constructed magically between India and Lanka.

A monk asked, "How could that have happened?"

Jairam explained, "Magic has science or some type of logic behind it. But, at times, that science or logic can be esoteric. For example, for people who do not understand how a hot air balloon functions, it flies by magic. Ramayana was written in a time when the information was spread through stories. To not burden the masses with the arcane science used behind the construction of the bridge, the stories relied on magic to drive the narrative. Since God knows all the science there is to know, he is the greatest scientist in the world. Until we discover how everything works on this planet, including how to reach God scientifically, God, especially in our holy books, is likely to be presented as the greatest magician."

8

Every month, we were updated on current events. One day, we heard about the indigo protests. In certain regions of East India, farmers were forced to cultivate indigo and paid only a fraction of the market price. Indigo cultivation without crop rotation had a negative impact on the yield of the land. When the farmers protested, the British banned the protests, considering the demand for indigo in England.

On a fateful day, more than 3,000 farmers gathered at a square in Calcutta to stage a peaceful protest, despite the ban. General Dier took the protest as an act of severe defiance and marched his troops to the square. Shocked by the presence of troops, the unhappy farmers shouted slogans against General Dier, who considered it appropriate to respond with a firm hand.

The General ordered his brave men to open fire at the unarmed protesters until they ran out of ammunition. From every direction, bullets flew at the farmers, who were left with no place or time to run or hide. When the ammunition finished performing its duty, only a handful of farmers had survived. Before the survivors grasped the horror, the bayonet was summoned to finish the job. The square witnessed the ghastly dance of death.

The event caused an uproar in the subcontinent, highlighting the brutal practices. This act of violence disturbed people in Britain too. However, a section in Britain hailed General Dier as a hero for displaying the courage to crush the bandits who were going to bring the empire (and indigo farming) down. This section raised thousands of pounds for General Dier, as a token of heartfelt appreciation.

The enterprising General Dier used the donation to run an unauthorized operation to smuggle out India's valuable antiques. In the process, he generated more money for his group. For Hindustanis, what was also shocking was that many of the soldiers who fired bullets at the unarmed farmers were Hindustanis themselves. Drafted into the British Army, they too viewed the poor farmers as expendables.

The news created an atmosphere of sadness at the monastery. Many monks meditated for long hours for peace, while skipping meals altogether. Since my training and education had completed, I was eager to take on a mission. It had been years since I last met General Dier on that unfortunate day in our village, when he had the camp set on fire. Many villagers, including my parents, had been reduced to ashes. The old wounds opened up like the floodgates to hell. Images of me standing as a bystander in horror flashed in front of my eyes. At that time, Hariram had pacified me to seal those wounds. I was no longer the boy whose wounds could be sealed. General Dier would have to pay his dues. From that day onward, Dier was on borrowed time.

9

Before I could go on missions, I was required to pass the martial arts test, involving three rounds of combat with different opponents. The first round consisted of a one-on-one battle. In the second and third rounds, the stakes increased as the test-taker battled against a team of three and five opponents respectively. The contestants were allowed to use weapons of their choice. The weapons were specially designed to not inflict fatal injuries.

The test had specific rules:
a) Do not make contact with opponent's neck and head
b) To win the combat, hit the torso or the back of the opponent, or make him part with his weapon
c) Utilize arms and legs, along with your weapons, to attack or defend

To pass, test-takers had to win all three rounds. I inquired with Jairam to learn if I could be scheduled for the test.

He responded, "We can schedule one next week. Would that work for you?"

On hearing that the test could be scheduled next week, I could not hide my excitement. "That would be great!"

"At dawn, a week from today, we will test you. I am expecting you to pass with flying colors."

"Thank you, Jairam."

While the test was conducted in a controlled environment, it was grueling, as the opponents were aware of the combatant's strengths and weaknesses, and therefore could strategize in advance. On the other hand, the test-taker would be kept in the dark about his opponents. In a way, the test was closer to a scenario where you walked into an ambush. Because you fought with new opponents in each round, the test was also a race where you ran the entire course, while your competitors ran a relay.

On the day of the combat, the windows of the upper level would be filled with monks peeking at the spectacle. Senior monks would be seated in the backyard. Despite displaying capability, not everyone was invited to take the test. Deep down, I realized that the Order of the Wolves had placed faith in me. It was an honor.

To prepare for the event, Toshiro Wakayama advised me to focus on my strengths, be aware of my surroundings, and use the conditions to my advantage. Many test-takers failed to advance not for lack of skills, but for the inability to finish the marathon. Round one, a one-on-one battle where both combatants started fresh, was contested on an equal footing. If you went past round one, you faced three fresh opponents, and if you were able to go past those three, you faced five fresh opponents. The difficulty level at each round increased exponentially.

Another challenge was the venue itself. The backyard ended at a precipice. There was no fence or marking to stop you from going over the cliff. If you went over the edge, the ride to the valley below was long enough to give enough time to recap the key moments of your life. The backyard was to the east; therefore, you had to be wary of sun rays hitting your eyes. A brief moment of blindness could end the dream.

In that week, I engaged myself in high-impact aerobics to condition my body to last nine opponents over three rounds. I also worked on sharpening my reflexes. More than anything else, a quicker kill in one round left you fresher for the next one. In the evenings, I performed meditation to hold my mind in focus, keeping both the mental and physical sides at their peak. The appointment with destiny was only a few hours away. On that afternoon, I spent time in the backyard to visualize the battle. I went to bed reimagining the best moments of my life.

At night, I dreamt of a wolf. Being chased through the forest by hunters, it arrived at a stream. The wolf had to make a decision—behind it were the hunters; in front of it, the stream. Since wolves are courageous, intelligent, and never give up, its mind was clear. It took a few measured steps backward, then ran toward the stream in full force to fling itself across.

10

At dawn, energy flowed through the monastery. As I entered the backyard, I heard cheers coming from the upper level. As I looked up, monks hung out of the windows to wave at me. The area around the huge bell was marked as the battleground. One of the monks, functioning as the head referee, asked me to stand near the bell. Two more monks were assisting him to oversee the contest. I did not have to wait long to find my opponents, as they entered the backyard to the welcoming cheer. Finally, the senior monks, including the Great One, Jairam, and Toshiro Wakayama made their way to the backyard. The monks at the upper level greeted them with a roar. The mood became festive at the monastery.

Once everyone was in their place, Jairam formally explained the rules. The Great One gave a short, encouraging speech to us. He highlighted the verse from the holy book Gita: "Do your karma without worrying about the results." With that, he declared the competition open. Jairam headed back to the section where the senior monks were seated. The referees marched in to take charge of the battleground.

My corner was called the bell's corner. The opponents stood diagonally across from me, near the main entrance to the backyard. Therefore, their corner was called the entrance corner. One of the referees walked up to me to examine my fitness. The other referee examined those at the entrance corner. The head referee waited for the result. As the two referees declared the combatants fit, the monastery roared again.

The referee at my corner provided me with two swords, one long and one short, specially designed for such events. Similarly, the referee at the entrance corner gave a couple of weapons to my first-round opponent. His choice of weapons was interesting. He was going to use a spear and a kusarigama, which is made up of a sickle and a metal chain with an iron ball attached at its far end. For the competition, the iron ball was replaced with wood, while the sickle and the spear were blunted to not cause major harm.

Considering that the contest could be won by a) hitting the opponent on his torso or back, or b) making the opponent lose one of his weapons, the monk had chosen his weapons wisely. He could use the reach of the spear to aim at my torso or back. The kusarigama provided capability in close-range combat, while the metal chain added reach. Both the weapons could also be used to attack my palms from a safe distance, forcing me to drop one of my weapons. The monk had used his preparation time effectively to strategize.

I began to create a plan. Toshiro Wakayama's advice flashed in my mind: a) play to your strengths, b) be aware of the surroundings, and c) use the conditions well. Since I was at the bell's corner on the easternmost tip of the monastery, I had a minor advantage. If I kept my back to the sun, the rays would hit the monk in his eyes, making it difficult for him to quickly anticipate my attacks. With both corners ready, the two referees nodded at the head referee, who sounded the bugle. Round one commenced.

Round One.

I examined my weapons and stretched my arms as I walked into a position where the sun was directly behind me. The monk took his position facing the sun. As we engaged in the duel, I raised the long sword at his eyes, not allowing him to focus on both of my swords at once. If he attacked with his spear, I would use the long sword to deflect the strike, either sideways or downward. The monk squinted as I stepped closer to deliver a blow on his torso. However, the monk saw this as an opportunity to fire the weight attached to the chain on the kusarigama at me. Since the long sword was raised for the attack and to deflect the spear, I caught the flying weight with the short sword. The weight wrapped around the sword, locking the weapon with the kusarigama. Both of us pulled the weapon in our left-hand with force, trying to create a momentum that snatched the opponent's tool away, but the weapons had not only securely locked themselves with each other but also us. Neither of us lost his weapon in this exercise. The battle moved its focus to the weapons in our right hands.

The locked-up position that we were engaged in shifted advantage to the monk, as now I was within his spear's reach, while he was out of my long sword's range. As expected, he thrust the spear at me. To counter that, I used my long sword to deflect it away. This exercise continued. Suddenly, I became aware of my surroundings. If I got closer, the monk would have difficulty in thrusting his spear. As I got closer, I also began to tighten the chain of the kusarigama with the short sword. The closer I got, the more frustrated the monk became, as his ability to strike me kept diminishing. Because of the rules of the combat, he could not release the kusarigama from his hand to try to salvage an advantage.

Out of desperation, the monk pushed the spear at me with all of his strength. I was able to dodge the blow by moving sideways. The momentum of the move carried the monk forward to provide me the opportunity to hit his grip on the spear with my long sword. The monk not only lost the spear, but also his balance. The pin-drop silence created by the tense battle was broken by roars from the monks on the upper level, signaling that I had survived round one.

Round Two.

In the next round, I had to beat three opponents who functioned as a team. This team had adopted a different strategy. The combatants were only going to use one weapon each—the talwar, which is a curved long sword. With each combatant using only one weapon, the chances of dropping a weapon were reduced too. Since I had to be the last man standing, the team could afford to lose men.

I analyzed their best options to attack me. One, they could charge at me together, front on. While I engaged with one, the others could target my back and torso. Two, they could form a triangle around me to attack from three different sides. I needed to get quick kills, as the more time I spent on the ground, the more advantage the opponents would gain.

I took my position at the bell's corner. The three opponents stood in a row, close to each other, with talwars raised in their hands at the entrance corner, suggesting that they were going for option one—an all-out attack, where all of them would charge toward me, creating the opportunity for one of them to succeed. With everyone, including the two referees, in position, the head referee sounded the bugle for the second time today.

The opponents rushed toward me, anticipating me to charge toward them as well, to meet at the center of the battleground. However, I did not run toward them. Once they gained speed, I ran sideways, to the corner on my left. This gambit by me forced the team to break their formation as they turned to charge toward me at the corner. When the opponents moved into the position in which I wanted them, I charged toward them. Since they had scattered, I could take them on one by one.

With full strength, I hit the talwar of the first opponent with my long sword, then I dodged the attack of the second opponent to hit his back with my short sword as he passed me. With the long sword, I blocked the attack of the third opponent and drove the short sword to his torso. In a matter of minutes, the battle was over. The first opponent had lost his sword, and the second and the third had been hit on their back and torso respectively. As I gathered myself to hang my swords next to me and bow, the monastery was still silent. It took time to realize that the battle was over as soon as it had begun. When the crowd grasped the situation, it thundered with a huge roar that could surely be heard at nearby villages. The roar continued to echo through the valley.

Round Three.

After what had transpired in round two, the five opponents of round three looked at me with newfound respect. They had realized the need to be at the top of their game or the contest could be over in minutes. The two wins had filled me with an added dose of confidence. If I could beat one, I could beat ten. If I could beat ten, I could beat a hundred. Suddenly, I felt like a wolf that had zeroed in on its prey. I could not wait to launch myself in round three. The monks at the upper level clapped in anticipation of an engrossing battle.

My opponents began to prepare for a military-like assault. They organized themselves in rows. At the front were two archers, and the second row had two monks with naginata, which is a long, wooden pole with a curved blade at its end. The third row had a monk who was armed with a talwar and a shield.

I reviewed the situation. The bell's corner and the entrance corner formed a diagonal. The two archers would run toward the sides to take positions to fire arrows at me. The two monks with naginata would charge toward me, while the monk with the talwar would follow them to get into a leverageable position. I had to create a situation where the archers could not get a clear shot at me. If they missed their shot, they could even hit their team members. I would have to take on both the monks with the naginatas at the same time, while observing the moves made by the monk with talwar, a wild card waiting to make a move as per how the cards would be dealt on the battleground. When everyone took their positions, the head referee sounded the third bugle of the day. As the sound blasted from the bugle, the wolf within me howled.

The bows ran sideways to take positions opposite of each other, the naginatas sped toward me, and the talwar kept its place behind the naginatas. Since a moving target is difficult to aim at, I ran toward the naginatas. The arrows zipped past me. As I got closer to the naginatas, I dived and rolled toward them, making it difficult for the naginatas to target my torso or back. Once I saw four legs, I crashed my swords into the two pairs of shins. The two monks tumbled and lost their naginatas. Immediately, I sprang back to my feet. Before the talwar could make any moves, I dived and rolled again, to arrive at his feet. With his hands spread out, holding the talwar and the shield, the monk was slow to react to the action on the ground. He felt the short sword touch his torso.

The five monks had expected the battle to be fought with me standing on my feet. I turned the conditions to take the combat to the legs level. This strategy also made it difficult for the archers to get a clear shot at me. With swift moves, I had taken three monks out of the equation. As I launched myself back to my feet, more arrows whizzed toward me. Using both the swords, I fended the arrows, while running to take a position between the two archers. Soon, I got into a position where the two archers would not only be shooting at me, but also at each other. The arrows from both sides missed the moving target, to rest at the two stationary ones. As the bows fell from their hands, round three ended. The wolf stopped at the huge bell and then turned toward the monastery, which had ignited with thunderous roars. The senior monks were on their feet, clapping their hearts out. It was as if destiny had picked the winner.

11

I was asked to report to the main meeting room on the ground floor, where I had met the Great One for the first time. The chairs across the round table were occupied by senior monks of the Order of the Wolves. From the distinguished chair with the tall back, the Great One gestured for me to enter the room. To his right and left were Jairam and Toshiro respectively. There was a vacant spot opposite of the Great One, where I was directed to sit.

The Great One spoke, "You have been approved to go on missions. Jairam is going to provide the details."

Jairam elaborated, "We have been receiving updates from Hariram on the activities of General Dier. He has created havoc in the East. No soul is safe from him. He is constantly protected by his troops and moves around the region; therefore, it is not easy to reach him. He has started a new venture, where he steals antiques from the native rulers and temples. These antiques are in demand around the world. The loot is smuggled out in batches by ships from Calcutta. The antiques are stored and prepared for shipping at a tribal village in the forest around River Teesta."

I inquired, "Why are the tribal helping General Dier?"

"The answer to that question is not straightforward. The tribal are under the influence of a man called Louis Short. He came in as a preacher with the troops but established his sect. By creating illusions and using science unknown to the tribal, he has brought the area under his spell. Reports suggest that he has resorted to cannibalism, which he terms as the sacrifice to the higher beings. Short and Dier have formed an evil nexus. Your task would be to infiltrate Short's gang. Via Short, arrange to meet Dier, and then destroy the set up."

"How do I infiltrate Short's gang?"

"We will provide you with antiques. You will allow yourself to be captured by the tribal. When the tribal learn that you have antiques, they will guide you to Short. Once Short sees you like a bird of his feather, he will ask you to flock with him together."

The Great One advised, "The mission is extremely dangerous. If Louis Short finds out about your motives, he will literally eat you. We have seen you grow up at this monastery and have no doubts about your capabilities, which were vindicated during the test. Our only concern is about your mental preparedness. Are you ready to take on such assignments?"

"Yes, sir."

The Great One looked to his left. "Toshiro has prepared a gift for you that, if used correctly, could make you invincible."

Toshiro smiled, "In the Higo province of Japan is the Dotanuki School, known to manufacture the best swords in the world. For the Order of the Wolves, they prepare special swords, which go beyond anything the world has ever imagined. I would like to present you with the Dotanuki Wolf, the long sword, and the Dotanuki Wolf Pup, the short sword."

Toshiro stood up from his chair to walk toward the table at a corner of the room. On the table were two boxes. One box was about four feet long, and the other, two feet. He put the small box on top of the big one and carried them to me. I stood up to accept the gifts and placed the boxes on the table. All of the monks in the room had a smile on their face. It was not often that they presented Dotanuki Wolf and Wolf Pup. It was a special occasion.

Toshiro opened the cases. As I looked inside, I was spellbound. The scabbard was in a matte royal blue. The tsuka (handle) in dark orange provided the contrast. The visual effect was like that of an orange sun in a blue sky. An engraved motif of a howling wolf served as the kashira.

Toshiro smoothly pulled the blade out of the scabbard and explained, "The blade material utilizes a mixture of advanced materials that we provide to Dotanuki. With appropriate force, it can cut a diamond, the hardest material known to us at this point. If you want to leave your mark, the wolf motif on the kashira can create an imprint on most surfaces. The blades can cut through bullets and arrows with ease. Be careful with it, as it takes a long time to harvest the advanced materials and manufacture the blade. You can say that the materials for the blade are provided by God."

Toshiro returned the two Dotanuki Wolves to their dens and headed back to his seat. Jairam said, "We will fly you to the Teesta, where you will meet Kaka Rai, who is a prince from one of the princely states. Kaka Rai will support you with the logistics and provide help."

"Why is the prince helping us?"

"Kaka Rai's state had to accept the conditions of the powerful British, but he wants them out of the region."

The Great One cautioned, "You should be circumspect of everyone you meet. Outside of the monastery, no one is aware of our location. Even though you would work with Kaka Rai, be careful about revealing any information about the Order. We provide him with information on a need-to-know basis for both his and our security. Only Hariram, who is from this monastery but carrying his mission from the village, is to be trusted completely."

"How can I contact the Order from the outside?"

Jairam answered, "We will be in the know of your actions. When you have an important question, we will be there for you. If you write to Hariram, ensure that the letter is cryptic. He may even accompany you on some missions. For some reason, if we need you here, we will send for you."

The Great One made the closing statement, "Be careful, son. Good luck. May the wolves guide you to your destiny!"

For the journey ahead, I was provided with items that I would need, including gold and money, and special fabrics to filter water. In one of the classes, I had learned to use various plants as food and medicine in an emergency, so that information could be useful in the forest.

While I was excited to be going on the mission, the thought of leaving the Wolf's Den made my heart heavy. I ruminated on how the years had passed. A few years ago, I had arrived at this place with just the Swordsman as my name; now, I was leaving the Wolf's Den with skills that had turned me into one.

At dawn, I began the trip to the tiny plateau. The monks waved goodbye as I walked out of the jaws of the wolf. I noticed that many monks were wiping their tears. Behind toughness hid softness in the heart of the Wolf's Den. Dressed in a dark-blue ninja outfit and with the two matching Dotanuki Wolves tucked around my waist, I boarded the hot air balloon. As we glided away, the Wolf's Den appeared to become miniature from the distance.

VINDICTA

12

East of Kanchenjunga and adjacent to the 7,100-meter-high Pauhunri, is the Teesta Kangse glacier. Teesta River originates from this glacier in Sikkim, and snakes through Bengal to merge with the Great Brahmaputra, which begins its journey at the Angsi Glacier and flows into the Bay of Bengal.

I took a morning dip in the cold Teesta and headed to the nearby temple of Lord Shiva. As is usual at temples, Lord Ganesha was seated to the left and Lord Hanuman stood at the right of the steps leading to the main hall. I took a lota each of milk and water and poured them over the Shivlinga, a tradition at Shiv temples. After the prayers, I rushed back to the river to meet Kaka Rai.

As I stood at the bank, admiring the scenic beauty, a sidewheeler riverboat headed in my direction. Its bow displayed the flag of Kaka Rai's princely state. Behind the flag sat a muscular figure with a narrow moustache, a long nose, and hair combed back. As the boat secured itself on the bank, the muscular figure jumped out of it and walked up to me.

"I am Kaka Rai, and you must be the Swordsman," he said, pointing at my two Dotanuki Wolves.

"Yes, I am the Swordsman. It is nice to meet you."

"It is nice to meet you as well."

After exchanging pleasantries, we got down to business.

"We have to head south, to the wildlife forest."

"How long does it take to reach there?"

"If we leave now, we should arrive by evening."

The sidewheeler began navigating the river. Kaka Rai explained the history of his state, which was left with no choice but to become a vassal of the British. If the state had resisted, the British would have toppled the king, his father. Kaka Rai, one of the princes in line to be crowned the next king, was responsible for the internal security of his state.

Kaka Rai continued, "We have respected and guarded our cultural heritage for centuries. But now, the antiques and articles that we respect are being stolen. Because of the thefts of religious idols, the citizens are upset, feeling that a catastrophe will strike the region if these acts are not stopped. The king has placed the issue on high priority."

The sidewheeler progressed slowly through the narrow river. While the river was calm, we were reminded of life around us by the bells sounding at temples at a distance and birds chirping in the forest. Kaka Rai invited me to have lunch on board, where he also served me one of their specialties, rose sorbet.

"We are about to enter the tribal land. The community lives deep inside the forest and follows its own unique customs. The tribal prefer to avoid contact with outsiders. Recently, they have increased their interactions with us. With the increase, the thefts in the state have gone up as well, which is surprising, considering they are not known to pursue material pleasures."

"What about Louis Short?"

"Short appears to have changed their behavior. It is hard to comprehend how he managed to do that. The tribal communities believe in living a simple life, so they do not gain much from such thefts. I am positive that the beneficiary is Short."

The sidewheeler pointed its bow toward the bank. Kaka Rai provided me with a royal antique to use as bait to get to Louis Short. He said, "We will wait for you in this area. If you are not back in a couple of days, we will enter the forest to search for you. Be careful."

13

I tracked through the thick forest on hilly terrain. Its canopy made the forest darker than what it should be in the evening. At certain points, I created markers to guide me back to the river. The forest was known to not only have wild elephants but also tigers. After making my way through the clusters of trees, I arrived at a trail created by elephants and followed it in the southeast direction. As it was getting dark, I was relying on my sense of smell and sound to navigate.

As I marched on, I sensed that I was not alone on the trail. Someone or something was tracking me at a distance. My goal was to run into the tribal and allow myself to get captured. Once the tribal learned about the royal antique, they would guide me to Short. The sound from the cracking twigs and dry leaves was now drawing closer. The force causing the twigs and dry leaves to crack had to be human. I tried to increase my pace but could not, as an acute pain gripped my body. My eyes closed and I collapsed.

Loud, rhythmic beats from drums woke me up. I managed to gather enough energy to pull myself out of a khatlo, a type of rope bed. As I walked out of the straw hut, a couple of tribal grabbed me and took me to a huge hut, which was decorated opulently like the inside of a sheik's tent. The two tribal threw me on a chair and left. Struggling to stay awake, I closed my eyes.

"You carry nice swords," said a soft, squeaky voice. I opened my eyes to find a square in front of me. He appeared square, as he was not only short but also large. His head was clean shaven, which exposed two natural bumps, spread apart like two tiny devil horns. As he smiled at me, his metal teeth flashed.

"I am Louis Short," he said, introducing himself.

"Why am I being held here?"

Short laughed in an unnatural manner. "You have been drugged. It appears as if the drug has had an impact on your memory, Swordsman."

Realizing that my cards were laid on the table, the answer to, "Who drugged me?" was obvious. What was not obvious was, "Why?"

The peculiar long nose walked into the glamorous hut. The lips under the narrow moustache opened: "We have administered the cure to the drug. You will be on your feet soon."

He continued, "The king is scheduled to host General Dier in a few days, where we will assassinate the king. By returning some of the religious antiques, including the royal one that I gave you, I will restore faith in the public and showcase my abilities. General Dier will propose me as the king, preferring to deal with me over other princes."

"How do you plan to get away with the assassination of the king?"

"The assassination will be carried out using your sword. I will stage a scene to apprehend you and then hand you over to General Dier, who will impart justice. I hope that I do not need to spell out the implications for you."

Despite my weak health, I gathered strength to deliver a punch to Kaka's face. He crashed to the floor. Kaka Rai was a wrestler. He got up on his feet and, with all his strength, put the sleeper hold on me. Louis Short interjected the action. "Careful, Kaka, we need him alive to take the fall for the assassination." Kaka Rai threw me back to my seat and left. Outside of the hut, the drums continued to play the rhythmic beats.

14

Short flashed his metal teeth at me and asked, "Do you know what I use them for?"

"How did a preacher end up with those teeth?"

"It is a long story, but since we have time, I will tell you."

Louis Short had spent time in China, where a section practiced cannibalism. Human beings were devoured as culinary delights and medicine. Eating an enemy was not uncommon as well. There were stories in China where nobles invited friends for dinner to serve them their servants, and of restaurants that specialized in human flesh. Short tasted these delights from time to time.

The East India Company produced poppy plants and processed them into opium. To escape legalities, private merchants were used to import opium into China. Looking at the opportunity, Short decided to venture into the opium business and targeted Chinese nobles. To hook the Chinese, he provided opium for free, then charged exorbitant prices. When he started to make good money, he expanded his operations.

A noble close to the Qing Dynasty investigated opium smuggling when his son suffered from addiction. Louis Short was apprehended, forced to consume large quantities of his opium, and banished from the village. He moved around the region aimlessly and suffered from dreadful diseases. He had heard about the use of Mumia powder, which contained mummified human flesh, as a remedy for various diseases in fifteenth-century Europe. Unable to find food and as a potential cure, he started eating human corpses, which led him to acquire the rare disease of rotting flesh. The corpses had transmitted an unknown bacterium to him. When his body started to rot, he sought refuge in forests.

He met a mysterious outcast, who advised him a cure: "A fresh human a month keeps the rotting disease away." Short thanked the outcast by eating him. He noticed that eating fresh humans reversed the rotting disease. Because of such inhumane consumption, he began to grow large. His short height made him appear square.

Once, he went for five weeks without eating a human, and that reactivated the rotting flesh disease. Desperate for the cure, he went to a village and killed. When the villagers caught him, they plucked out all his teeth. Just as he was about to be put to death, a British team rescued and shipped him to India.

In India, he was introduced to General Dier, who used him for his antique business. Kaka Rai had made a secret pact to support Dier if he was made the king of his state. He had given out state secrets to the British, which had enabled the British to turn his state into a vassal. As a part of the plan, Kaka Rai brought Short to the tribal land and presented him as a magician. Short performed tricks that he had learned in China. Eventually, Short started to control the tribal. Kaka Rai and his bandits carried out the antique thefts and framed the tribal. Now, this evil nexus was only a few days away from assassinating the king. The princely state and the tribal were at peril.

15

Louis Short, Kaka Rai, and his bandits marched me back to the sidewheeler. My hands were tied behind my back and I had a rope around my neck. The rope around my neck was controlled by Kaka Rai. I was seen as an animal pulled to get slaughtered. I inquired, "Why did you bring me all the way to the forest to capture me when I was already on the boat?"

"The drug takes time to show its effect. We were on our way to pick up Louis Short anyway and the forest serves as our holding place," said Kaka Rai.

Louis Short carried my swords and commented, "We use guns, not such toys."

Kaka Rai remarked, "He is a Hindustani ninja."

Short laughed out loud in his unnatural manner. "Hindustani ninja!"

The group burst out in laughter at the joke. Kaka Rai added fuel to the fun, "Before you even attempt to wield your sword, you will get killed by a bullet."

Short said, "If you were not required to take the fall for the assassination, you would have been my dinner. I will miss not knowing how a Hindustani ninja tastes!"

Kaka Rai roared with laughter. "Maybe we can ask General Dier to give you a piece from him."

"General Dier plans to torture him to learn about the location of the Order of the Wolves. I can make him talk in minutes."

"Why should we waste time on those clowns, who believe that they can bring us down with this fool?" With that comment, Kaka Rai pulled the rope around my neck. One of the bandits attacked me from behind to make me fall on the ground. Once I fell, the bandits gathered to kick me from all sides.

"Enough. We need him to walk to the sidewheeler. Unless all of you want to carry him," Kaka ordered. The group once again burst out in laughter at my plight. One of the bandits could not resist kicking my face, as he wanted more fun. They put me back on my feet as we stepped into the sidewheeler. They considered themselves invincible.

With a gun on my head, my hands were untied and the rope around my neck removed. I was laid in the supine position on the deck, with both my arms and legs stretched out and secured to the floor. The confident Short casually placed my swords on the deck and winked. "They will make you feel at home."

As the sidewheeler floated northward, the sun hit the deck. Kaka Rai enjoyed the situation that I was in. He was a man who derived pleasure from slow tortures, where the victims were both mentally and physically disintegrated.

The sidewheeler cruised on the narrow river. With the effects of the drug wearing off, I was regaining my strength. I closed my eyes to find the Great One in the darkness. I recalled in my mind, *"We fight not only the British, but also the Hindustanis who help the British to subjugate other Hindustanis."* I realized that the Hindustanis who supported the imperial forces were worse. They used the British to gain short-term benefits. The British happily obliged and took the bigger piece of the cake.

Had the Great One known that I would be betrayed? He had warned me about not trusting anyone. Was this a part of my learning process? To observe the evil and the betrayal from close quarters? The Order of the Wolves had entrusted me with this important mission, which now acquired a new dimension, with the planned assassination of the king of the princely state. I could not let the Order of the Wolves down. To stop the evil nexus, I would have to gather all my strength, and more importantly, show no mercy to the enemies. I was not even sure anymore if such people could be classified as human beings.

 Rhythmic beats from the drums echoed through the tribal land as dark clouds hid the sun and rain hit the deck. At a distance, I heard the wolves howl. I continued to meditate, feeling a different kind of energy circulate through my body. It was as if the wolves had transferred their powers to me.

I pulled my arms and legs with all my strength to break the ropes, stood up, stretched casually, and walked to collect my swords, which an overconfident Short had left on the deck. Shell-shocked by the proceedings, Kaka Rai's mouth opened wide. He even rubbed his eyes to make sure that he wasn't dreaming. I took the two Dotanuki Wolves out of their sheaths. All fifteen men on the sidewheeler stopped their activities and rushed to where I was on the deck. They no longer appeared invincible.

Kaka Rai regained his composure. As his confidence came back, he motioned the others to stand at their positions. Despite the need to make me take the fall for the assassination, he knew he could no longer keep me alive. It was them versus me. With just one option remaining, the wicked smile returned on his face as he took his gun out and aimed at me.

"Guns versus swords, Hindustani ninja." He mocked me by wielding his gun like a sword.

I opened my arms. With the long sword and the short sword in my right and left hands respectively, I rushed toward him. He aimed at my chest and fired. As the bullet left his gun, I bent to slide on my knees. The wet deck quickly brought me near Kaka Rai's legs. With a smooth swing of my swords, Kaka Rai was left without his legs. Louis Short froze, as if he had seen the devil.

With their leader without legs struggling on the floor, six bandits fetched their talwars and ran toward me. I stepped back to allow them to come closer. These were the mighty men who had kicked me around in the forest. As I glanced in their eyes, I saw fear. With my long sword, I hit the gunwale next to me to crash it into pieces. The bandits had never seen anything like that before. They received the message, dropped their weapons, and moved to the side, clearing the path to Louis Short.

As I walked closer to Short, his eyes widened. He looked at the toys in my hands and realized that he was powerless. I beckoned him to come to me. He labored on his way. I pointed at Kaka Rai with my sword and asked Short to eat him.

The sidewheeler had drums onboard; therefore, I asked the bandits to play them. Those without drums had to tap on the deck to create beats. As the beating and tapping began, Short realized that this was his last meal, so he might as well enjoy it. Kaka Rai watched in horror as Short flashed his metal teeth.

These were the fifteen men that had appeared invincible not so long ago. Thirteen of them were either playing drums or tapping their feet on the deck, one lay on the floor without his legs, waiting to be eaten, and one was going to enjoy his last meal.

As Short approached, Kaka Rai begged to not be eaten alive. Life had turned the tables on Kaka Rai. Here was a man who was used to others begging to him for mercy.

I shouted at the bandits, "If the drums or the tapping stops, I will cut off your arms and legs." The beats grew louder. Short sat down next to Kaka Rai, who was now pleading with horror. Short drooled as he eyed the peculiar nose.

The cries from Kaka Rai matched the sounds of the beats. After a while, the rhythm from the drums and tapping continued, but the cries from Kaka Rai stopped. Short was drenched in blood. There was a calmness in his demeanor. After turning into a cannibal, Short saw himself on the path to become the next devil. His goal was never to remain human. He had hoped to meet the devil in the forest and request him to be turned into one too. Now, he acted as if he had finally found the devil. He felt sorry for not recognizing me earlier. He thought maybe the devil works by creating illusions. Today, he had been rewarded for his persistence. His long-time wish had come true. The devil was here, to turn into one too. He thought that he must follow the ritual and pass the devil's test.

I asked Short to eat his own arms. Without hesitation, he obliged. I pointed my sword at his mouth and commanded him to eat it. He smiled at the ritual. As he bit the sword, his metal teeth crashed out. I still kept my sword pointed at his mouth. He tried again. This time, his chin and nose separated into two. I took the pommel of the short sword to paste the howling wolf motif on the forehead of the two bodies, which could not be classified as human beings.

The rhythmic beat from the drums and tapping feet continued, reminding me that today was not the day for mercy. I asked the thirteen men to stand in a single file and raise their left hands. As they obeyed my command, in a flash, I ran through their hands. The thirteen left hands fell on the decks to a cacophony of cries of agony from their owners, disturbing the forest. The solace for the bandits was that their lives had been spared and that they had the opportunity to use them properly from now on.

17

With Kaka Rai and Louis Short out of the way, the king of the princely state was safe. Unlike my village, that state would remain under its own flag. I made my way up north to the village to meet Hariram. It had been years since I last saw him. I wondered if he would recognize me.

I reached the village in the evening. It was also the time when Hariram told stories at the huge, old tree. A part of me still wanted to listen to those stories, so I rushed down the cobbled streets to the village square where the huge, old tree was.

I was just in time for the session. The kids were seated around the tree, facing a familiar figure in an orange robe, parked gracefully on his throne. I took a seat with the kids. Hariram smiled at me and understood that I wanted to listen to what he had to say.

Hariram began, "The British are using the Andaman and Nicobar Islands as prisons to exile political prisoners. Since the 1857 mutiny, many independence activists have been sent to the prisons on those Islands, which are also known as Kala Pani (Black Water)."

One of the kids asked, "Are conditions harsh on Kala Pani?"

"The islands are isolated, so information coming out of them is sparse. But I have heard of prisoners being chained to work on difficult projects. Since the independence movement is gaining momentum, the British are building a cellular jail there to accommodate more prisoners."

After the class was dispersed, Hariram walked up to me. "Swordsman, you have grown up!"

I updated him on Kaka Rai and Louis Short, and that I was going after General Dier, who, after learning about the events on the sidewheeler, had retreated to one of the tea garden bungalows at the northeast of the village for a short holiday to clear his mind.

"I will be heading to the tea garden bungalow tomorrow."

"I will join you."

"Hariram, you know what Kaka Rai and Louis Short tried to do to me. It is dangerous out there."

"Don't worry, son. Let me show you something."

I stayed at Hariram's house. After dinner, Hariram showed me his bow and arrow. On the tip of the bow was the motif of the howling wolf. Since the Order of the Wolves had provided the bow to Hariram, he must have been an expert archer.

Hariram confirmed, "I do not need to get close to the enemies."

"What do you plan to do?"

"I will take care of General Dier's security outside the bungalow. You deal with whatever is inside."

It appeared as if the camp's fire was still burning inside Hariram. In the morning, we rode our horses to the bungalow.

18

We surveyed the area. A dozen men protected a holidaying General Dier. Most of them were stationed outside the house. We decided to make the move when General Dier retired to bed.

The lights inside the bungalow began to turn off. Only the living area and the porch were lit. Hariram nodded, signaling that it was time for me to go, while preparing his bow. As I ran toward the bungalow, the soldiers outside the bungalow started to fall to the ground, one by one. By the time I reached the house, the area had been cleared of soldiers without any noise. Hariram was, indeed, a master archer.

The bungalow was one story, with an integrated porch all around it. The house stood on a hill, providing it with unobstructed views of the scenic landscape. One of the sides of the house faced a cliff, facing Kanchenjunga. Except for the living area, inside of the house was dark. The porch was sparsely lit up. It appeared as if the occupants had confidently predicted no action during the night.

I used my short sword to cut the glass from a section on one of the windows, then I punched through the hole to unlatch the window and entered the empty room. It was a library, where General Dier had been reading. Once he had finished reading, he had switched the lights off and retired to his bedroom. I tiptoed to the door, which opened into the living area. The two British soldiers in the living area were relaxed and unaware of what had happened to their colleagues outside and to the library inside.

To get to General Dier's room, I would have to go past the two soldiers. Another option was to go around the porch and enter Dier's room from the outside. As I evaluated the next steps, the door of the room opposite of the library opened. General Dier walked out of it and asked one of the two soldiers to fetch one of the soldiers from the outside. I knew of the fate awaiting the soldier if he stepped out.

The soldier obeyed the orders, opened the door, stepped onto the porch, noticed the carnage outside, felt the shock, and let out a loud cry. The moment he had stepped out of the house, a missile had left the bow on its way to him, and just when he had let the cry out, he was struck by the missile. He fell on the ground to join his colleagues.

Inside the house, General Dier and the soldier realized the situation that they were in. As I stepped into the living room, General Dier gave the obvious order, "Stop him," and rushed inside his room to get his weapon.

The soldier drew his gun out. I stretched myself and opened up my arms with the two swords. The soldier fired. I used my sword to deflect the rocketing bullet heading toward my chest. The soldier was shocked by my lightening reflexes and the fact that there were no dents on the sword. He realized that his opponent was not ordinary. Unable to decide his next move, the soldier ran outside just as General Dier walked back into the room with his weapon. The panicked soldier had overlooked what awaited him outside. A missile struck a soldier again.

General Dier knew that he was trapped. He asked, "Who are you?"

"I am the Swordsman of the Order of the Wolves. You killed my parents in the camp's fire at the village. On behalf of all the Hindustanis who have suffered because of you, I am here to punish you for your sins."

I threw my short sword at his hand holding the weapon. Both the hand and the weapon flew to rest on the ground. As the hand dislodged from his body, General Dier's eyes widened with shock and his lips parted to yell out his agony. He rushed out in panic too. However, no missile struck him. Hariram had left General Dier in my hands.

As General Dier began to run toward the forest, the silence of the night was broken by howls at a distance. The wolves had sensed that one of their kind was on to its prey. I mounted my horse to follow Dier.

General Dier ran, slowed down, caught his breath, glanced back to find me following him, widened his eyes in terror, and ran again. The process continued for a while, till he ran out of energy. Since he could not run any longer, I decided to give him a ride.

I galloped my horse at him, snatched him by his collar, and dragged him along the ground. As the horse ran faster, Dier's feet brushed the ground harder until a point came where he could no longer feel them. The images of all the tortures that he had carried out flashed before his eyes. Deep inside the forest, the wolves continued to howl. My eyes shone yellow.

Ahead of us was a large tree. Dier saw it with whatever senses were still active within him. He knew what was coming but had lost the ability to react. Like his victims, he had accepted his fate. With a loud thud, Dier crashed into the tree. My eyes turned brown again.

Even though it had been a difficult night, we were glad that the mission was completed. Justice had prevailed. On our way back to the village, Hariram recalled one of his adventures as the Archer.

Epilogue

Intrigued by what I had learned in the memoirs, I decided to prolong my stay at the ancient monastery. I dug deeper to see if I could discover more records. When I finally gave up on finding more documents, my eyes fell on a peculiar cabinet at a corner. The cabinet blended in with the furniture in the library, except for one detail—it had the motif of a wolf on one of its corners. I rushed to examine the motif in detail.

The motif looked normal, except that the eyes of the wolf had a sparkle. I discovered that the eyes could be pushed. However, my attempts to push each eye to open a secret did not yield results. If the eyes of the wolf motif were designed to be pushed, it had to have a purpose. When nothing worked, I had a Eureka moment—what if I pushed both the eyes together? When I did that, the bottom part of the cabinet opened. Inside the cabinet were additional pages of the memoirs.

But why were these documents hidden? As I read through them, the hair on my body rose. A chill passed through my body as I learned about this villain with six toes. Like God, did the Devil take the form of man too? Would it be right to bring the information in these memoirs out?

Zenodamus

www.zenodamus.wordpress.com

ⁱ In the late nineteenth century, the world population was around 1.6 billion. In 2050, it is estimated to cross 10 billion.

www.ingramcontent.com/pod-product-compliance
Lightning Source LLC
Chambersburg PA
CBHW021334060726
47591CB00006B/2005